Family Soccer

D1558854

written by
Diana Geddes

illustrated by
Kate Salley Palmer

My family played soccer in the backyard.

Mom hit the ball with her head.

My brother hit
the ball with
his chest.

My sister hit
the ball with
her shoulder.

Dad hit the ball
with his stomach.

I hit the ball
with my knee.

Mom kicked
the ball with
her foot.

Mom made a Goal!